♡ Eva Sees a Ghost ♡

Read more
OWL DIARIES
books!

OWL DIARIES

♡ Eva Sees a Ghost ♡

Rebecca Elliott

BRANCHES

SCHOLASTIC INC.

For Toby. My little Ghostbuster. —R.E.

Special thanks to Eva Montgomery.

No part of this work may be reproduced, stored in a retrieval system, or transmitted in any form or by any means, electronic, mechanical, photocopying, recording, or otherwise, without written permission of the publisher. For information regarding permission, write to Scholastic Inc., Attention: Permissions Department, 557 Broadway, New York, NY 10012.

Library of Congress Cataloging-in-Publication Data

Elliott, Rebecca, author.
Eva sees a ghost / by Rebecca Elliott.
pages cm. – (Owl diaries ; 2)
Summary: When Eva Wingdale sees something large and white flying above her she is convinced that it is a ghost, although most of the other owls just laugh at her—until something large and heavy and white lands on the school roof.
ISBN 0-545-78783-1 (pbk. : alk. paper) – ISBN 0-545-78784-X (hardcover : alk. paper) – ISBN 0-545-78787-4 (ebook) – ISBN 0-545-78790-4 (eba ebook)
1. Owls—Juvenile fiction. 2. Belief and doubt—Juvenile fiction. 3. Elementary schools—Juvenile fiction. 4. Diaries—Juvenile fiction. [1. Owls—Fiction. 2. Ghosts—Fiction. 3. Belief and doubt—Fiction. 4. Schools—Fiction. 5. Diaries—Fiction.] I. Title.
PZ7.E45812Ev 2015
[Fic]—dc23

2014041324

ISBN 978-0-545-78784-0 (hardcover) / ISBN 978-0-545-78783-3 (paperback)

10 9 8 7 6 5 4   15 16 17 18 19 20/0

Printed in the U.S.A.   23
First Scholastic printing, June 2015

Book design by Marissa Asuncion
Edited by Katie Carella

♡ Table of Contents ♡

1

♥ Hello! ♥

Sunday

Hello Diary,

It's me – Eva Wingdale! Did you miss me? I bet you did!

I love:

Drawing

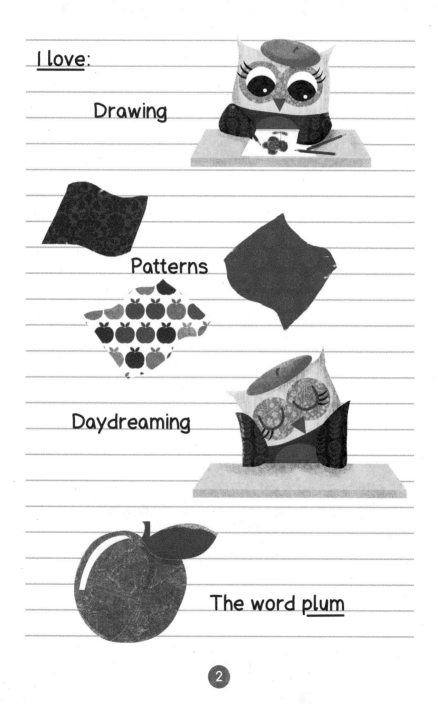

Patterns

Daydreaming

The word plum

Funky hats

QUESTIONNAIRE
1. What is your name?
2. What's your favorite color?
3. What's your favorite food?
4. How tall are you?
5. How fast can you fly?

Questionnaires

My friends

Being super excited!

I DO NOT love:

My brother Humphrey's
horrible singing

Sue Clawson
("Meany McMeanerson")

The color gray

Washing my feathers

Being scared

Squirrels

Mom's caterpillar
sandwiches

Feeling lonely

Here is my family:

Dad

Mom

Baby Mo

Humphrey

Me

And here is my pet bat, Baxter!

He's so cuddly!

We can fly.

We sleep in the daytime.

We're awake in the nighttime!

And we live in trees.

I live at Treehouse 11 on Woodpine Avenue in Treetopolis.

My BEST friend is Lucy Beakman. She lives in the tree next door.

We have sleepovers all the time! Our next one is on Sunday – one week from today! Yay!

Lucy has a pet lizard named Rex. Rex is Baxter's best friend, too!

Lucy and I go to Treetop Owlementary. Here is a photo of our class:

Miss Featherbottom   Carlos
Zac   Macy   Lilly

my class

Sue   Jacob   Lucy   Me   George   Zara

I'm off to school now. Talk to you tomorrow, Diary!

♡ No One Believes Me ♡

Monday

Miss Featherbottom read our class a spooky story tonight.

It was a dark and stormy day . . .

Everyone was in a flap after Miss Featherbottom finished reading!

But Lucy and I were TOO excited about our AMAZING SLEEPOVER to be scared by a silly story. (Well, maybe we were just a tiny bit scared.)

At lunch, we planned our sleepover activities.

<u>Things we'll do at Sunday's sleepover</u>:

- Bake worm muffins

- Braid beads into our feathers

- Draw pictures of kittens wearing hats

- Give our pets makeovers

- Stay up for a daytime snack

The sleepover was all I could think about on the flight home. I was flying with Lucy, Carlos, Sue, and Zac when it happened! I SAW A GHOST! There was a white, shimmery blur floating right above us!

But by the time they looked up, the ghost was gone.

Everyone laughed.

Then Sue said something not so nice.

Oh, stop flapping, Eva.
You just made that up.
Everyone knows ghosts
aren't real!

So now you can see why I call Sue
"Meany McMeanerson"! She is SO mean!

This ghost WAS real. I didn't make it up! (This is not like the time I didn't do my math homework because I said I was allergic to the number two. I totally made that up.)

I was upset that no one believed me.

Then Lucy whispered in my ear.

I believe you, Eva.

She really is the best friend in the whole **OWLIVERSE**.

When I got home, I told Humphrey about the ghost. He laughed.

Did the ghost go <u>boo</u> or <u>ooo</u>? If it didn't say <u>boo</u> or <u>ooo</u>, then it wasn't a real ghost.

He's such a squirrel-head. Maybe he's right, though. The ghost didn't go <u>boo</u>. Or <u>ooo</u>.

I guess Miss Featherbottom's spooky story <u>could</u> have made my imagination go a bit crazy.

But I really did see <u>something</u>, Diary! So I need to prove to everyone that there <u>is</u> a ghost in Treetopolis. My mission:

Find the ghost!

♡ It Chased Me! ♡

Tuesday

Hi Diary,

I saw the ghost again tonight!! This time, I was by myself near the Old Oak Tree when I heard a twig <u>snap</u>.

A spooky, silent white creature swooped <u>out of nowhere</u>! And it started chasing me!

I flew through the trees. It was right on my tail feathers!

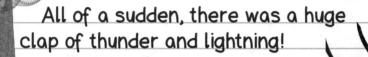

All of a sudden, there was a huge clap of thunder and lightning!

I flew down to the ground – then up, up almost to the stars. And still it chased me!

I think the ghost wanted to eat me. (I did eat lots of yummy berries and bugs tonight. So I guess I would taste pretty good.)

I dived into a swamp to hide.
I waited there for a bit.

Then I flew home as fast as my
swampy wings could carry me.

Now I <u>KNOW</u> I'm not making anything up! This ghost is NOT in my imagination. It is REAL.

(I once imagined I was Queen of the Furry Fairy People. That wasn't real. I can tell the difference.)

25

I've put Baxter
on guard-bat duty.

I'm going to take a bath. Then I'm
going to go talk to my friends and
neighbors. I'll ask if they have seen
anything strange in the forest. I can't be
the <u>only</u> one who has seen the ghost.

I love questionnaires. So I'm going
to give each owl a list of questions to
answer.

Here is what I've come up with:

QUESTIONNAIRE

1. What is your name? _____

2. How smart are you?
   ☐genius ☐smart ☐average ☐squirrel

3. Where do you live?
   ☐forest floor ☐swamp ☐tree trunk
   ☐nest ☐barn

4. Have you SEEN anything strange or scary in the forest (apart from my brother Humphrey)? _____

5. Have you HEARD anything strange or scary in the forest (apart from Humphrey's windy bottom)? _____
   _____
   _____
   _____

6. Do you believe in ghosts?
   ☐yes ☐no ☐maybe

I'll let you know how things go, Diary. It has been a long night and I'm off to bed. Good day.

♡ Proof ♡

Wednesday

Hi Diary,

    I gave questionnaires to every owl I could find — thirty-five in all! Then Lucy and I collected them back.

Most of the forms look something like Humphrey's:

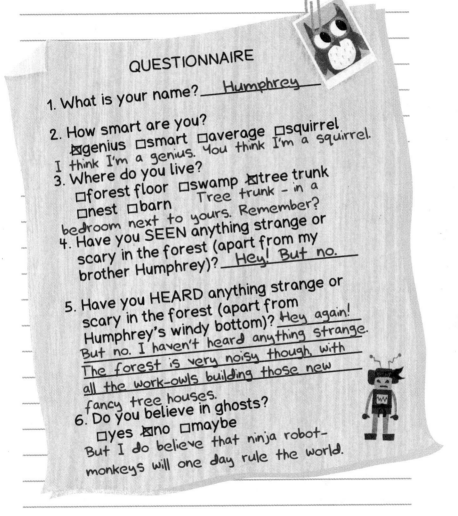

QUESTIONNAIRE

1. What is your name? __Humphrey__

2. How smart are you?
   ☒genius ☐smart ☐average ☐squirrel
   I think I'm a genius. You think I'm a squirrel.

3. Where do you live?
   ☐forest floor ☐swamp ☒tree trunk
   ☐nest ☐barn   Tree trunk - in a
   bedroom next to yours. Remember?

4. Have you SEEN anything strange or
   scary in the forest (apart from my
   brother Humphrey)? __Hey! But no.__

5. Have you HEARD anything strange or
   scary in the forest (apart from
   Humphrey's windy bottom)? __Hey again!__
   But no. I haven't heard anything strange.
   The forest is very noisy though, with
   all the work-owls building those new
   fancy tree houses.

6. Do you believe in ghosts?
   ☐yes ☒no ☐maybe
   But I do believe that ninja robot-
   monkeys will one day rule the world.

Okay, so most owls did not see or hear anything strange. But three owls DID!

Nanny Beakin said she heard <u>whooshing</u> sounds coming from very high up — above the trees! (That's higher than most of us fly. IT MUST BE THE GHOST!)

Mr. Twitteroo said he found this white feather outside his house. I think the ghost has EATEN someone and this is all that is left! (It cannot be anyone I know because I don't know anyone with white feathers.)

Jacob said he heard a <u>boo</u> sound. Then he said it may have been a cow saying <u>moo</u>. I like Jacob. He is a bit of a squirrel-head, though.

This information is helpful. But it is still not enough to prove that the ghost is real.

I have to get some rest now. I'll need lots and lots of energy for our BIG GHOST HUNT tomorrow!

♥ Boo! ♥

Oh, Diary!
Tonight was NOT a good night at school.

I was nightdreaming about being a famous ghost hunter.

Then Miss Featherbottom came into class. She has a very LOUD voice.

When she **HOOTED**, I fell off my chair!

Hello, class!

It was so embarrassing. Everyone laughed. Sue called me a scaredy-owl.

Then, at lunchtime, I was eating my **SLUGERONI AND CHEESE** when Humphrey snuck up behind me.

I threw my lunch into the air.

Everyone laughed again. Then they ALL started talking about how I <u>think</u> I saw a ghost.

They all think I'm a squirrel-head.
I HAVE to prove to them that I didn't
make up the ghost.

I'm so glad this stinky school night
is over. Now Lucy and I are going to go
on our ghost hunt. We just put on cool
ghost-hunter outfits. Look!

Now we're ready. I'll let you know
how it goes. Wish us luck, Diary!

♥ The Ghost Hunt ♥

Lucy and I flew to the Old Oak Tree after school yesterday. We sat there and waited.

And waited.

And ate our snacks.

And waited some more.

At one point, Grandpa Owlfred flew past. He's building the fancy new owl tree houses.

We chatted about our sleepover while we waited.

We waited some more. Then Lucy said something surprising.

How could Lucy leave me?! Now NO ONE believes me. Not even my best friend! I hope you still believe me, Diary!

After Lucy left, I waited some more. I sat by the Old Oak Tree until it was almost daylight. I felt sleepy.

THEN . . .

WHOOSH!

The white ghostly figure swooped right past me! It made a booming <u>boo</u> sound!! (Well, it may have been a loud <u>hoot</u> sound or even a <u>moo</u> sound. It was hard to tell. But I definitely heard an <u>oooo</u> noise!)

I was SO scared, Diary! And my wings were shaking SO much that I could hardly hold Lucy's camera.

The photo came out blurry. But at least I finally have PROOF that the ghost is real!

I've never been as scared as I was last night, Diary. I don't know how I got <u>any</u> sleep!

I'm going to take this photo to school tonight. I'll show everyone that I <u>am</u> telling the truth!

7

♥ Spooky School! ♥

Saturday

I carried my ghost photo into school last night.

Treetop Owlementary

Soon, it was time for show-and-tell.

Who would like to share first?

I flew to the front of the class.

I have something to show!

What is that?

It's a photo of the ghost! I saw it <u>again!</u>

It doesn't look like a ghost.

It's a ghost!

Listen, if Eva says that's a picture of a ghost, then that's what it is. She doesn't make things up!

Thanks, Lucy!

I showed the photo again. But the other owlets just laughed.

I flew back to my seat.

Miss Featherbottom asked everyone to quiet down. Then she put her wing around me.

Your photo is blurry, Eva. That makes it hard to see what this is a picture of. I love that you have such an amazing imagination though! That gives me an idea!

Let's all tell our <u>best</u> scary stories. And whoever tells the scariest story gets to ring Barry the Bell!

Everyone loves ringing Barry the Bell. So everyone wanted to tell a scary story.

George told a story about zombie squirrels.

Macy told one about giant spiders.

And Lilly was halfway through telling a story about fire-breathing dragons when . . .

There was a LOUD noise on the roof!

We all went quiet. Our beaks were wide open. Our wings were shaking. Even our teacher looked scared.

BAM!

There it was again! Something BIG was up on the roof!

I rushed to the window and opened it. I stuck my beak out to try to look up at the roof. Everyone crowded around.

We saw two ghostly white beasts swooping high above us.

Everyone started saying they were sorry. Then Lucy tugged on my wing.

Eva, I'm sorry I didn't believe you the <u>whole</u> time.

That's okay. I probably wouldn't have believed me, either!

I'm so happy Lucy believes me again!

Miss Featherbottom came back. She said there was nothing to worry about.

We all looked at one another, but nobody said anything. Would she believe us if we told her we saw ghosts?

We were all quiet. Then Sue raised her wing.

Um, Miss Featherbottom, we think Eva should get to ring the bell. Her ghost story was the scariest!

I couldn't believe it! Sue said I should ring the bell! I smiled at her. And I rang that bell as loudly as I could!

Bing-a-Ling-a-Ling!

At lunch, we came up with a plan.

Let's **all** go on a Treetop Owlementary Ghost Hunt tomorrow!

Yes! Together, we'll catch the ghosts!

We'll need some ghost-catching tools!

Let's make a ghost-hunting kit after school!

So, Diary, the good news is: Everyone believes me now. But the bad news is: Treetopolis is haunted!

Uh-oh! I have to go! It's almost time for the ghost hunt!

♥ The Ghost Group ♥

Sunday

Yesterday, we all went on the Treetop Owlementary Ghost Hunt. We took our ghost-hunting kit to the Old Oak Tree.

Macy and Zac brought a huge ghost-catching net.

George and Lilly brought a big
water-balloon-throwing slingshot.

Zara and Carlos brought
binoculars for looking far away.

Jacob and Sue brought a blanket for
us all to hide under.

And Lucy and I brought Ghost
Hunter costumes for everyone.

We were ready!

Carlos and Zara flew to the top of the tree. The rest of us waited under the blanket.

Suddenly, Zara saw something.

Quick! One of the ghosts is coming this way!

George loaded the slingshot. Lilly pulled it back.

ATTACK!

The huge white ghost whoosed past us. SPLAT! Lilly and George missed.

The beast flew toward us again.

WHOOSH!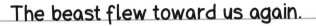

Macy and Zac threw
the net. It landed right on
top of the ghost!

We got it!!

Everyone else was
still hiding under the blanket.
So I was the only one who
finally got a good look at the
ghost. But it was too late.

Diary, it was so **HOOTINGLY** horrible!

I flew toward the net.

The other owlets were too scared to come out from under the blanket. They're such scaredy-owls.

But Lucy flew over. She helped me untangle the net.

The ghost wasn't a ghost at all . . .

Then four more white owls swooped down from the trees. They landed next to Lucy and me.

The big, white snowy owl started to laugh. He laughed so hard he was holding his belly.

Our classmates had questions for the snowy owls, too.

By the way, I'm Eva. This is my best friend, Lucy.

It's lovely to meet you. I'm Kiera.

Hi!

Our classmates all met Kiera.

Hello.

Glad you're not a ghost.

Then Kiera's family and the other owlets flew off.

This was the best ghost hunt ever!

Just then, I had the best idea ever! I whispered it to Lucy.

Lucy stepped forward.

Kiera, Eva and I are having a sleepover tomorrow. Would you like to come, too?

I'd love to!

Now I need to go get ready for our big sleepover. Lucy, Kiera, and I are going to have the best sleepover ever!

So, Diary, I thought I'd found a ghost. But, really, I'd found something much better: a new friend.

Rebecca Elliott was a lot like Eva when she was younger: She loved making things and hanging out with her best friends. Now that Rebecca is older, not much has changed — except that her best friends are her husband, Matthew, and their children Clementine, Toby, and Benjamin. She still loves making things, like stories, cakes, music, and paintings. But as much as she and Eva have in common, Rebecca cannot fly or turn her head all the way around. No matter how hard she tries.

Rebecca is the author of JUST BECAUSE and MR. SUPER POOPY PANTS. OWL DIARIES is her first early chapter book series.

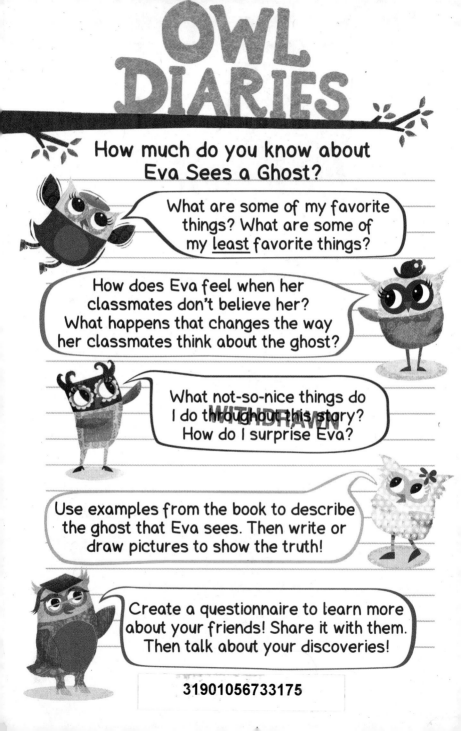

OWL DIARIES

How much do you know about Eva Sees a Ghost?

What are some of my favorite things? What are some of my <u>least</u> favorite things?

How does Eva feel when her classmates don't believe her? What happens that changes the way her classmates think about the ghost?

What not-so-nice things do I do throughout this story? How do I surprise Eva?

Use examples from the book to describe the ghost that Eva sees. Then write or draw pictures to show the truth!

Create a questionnaire to learn more about your friends! Share it with them. Then talk about your discoveries!